Highway To HORROR

Publisher's Cataloging-in-Publication Data
(Prepared by The Donohue Group, Inc.)

   Route 666. Volume one : highway to horror / Writer: Tony Bedard ; Penciler: Karl Moline ;
Inker: John Dell ; Colorist: Nick Bell.

   p. : ill. ; cm.

   Spine title: Route 666. 1 : highway to horror

   ISBN: 1-931484-56-2

1. Cassie Starkweather (Fictitious character)--Fiction. 2. Graphic novels. 3. Psychic ability--
Fiction. 4. Supernatural--Fiction. 5. Horror comic books, strips, etc. 6. Horror fiction.
I. Bedard, Tony. II. Moline, Karl. III. Dell, John. IV. Bell, Nick. V. Title: highway to horror
VI. Title: Route 666. 1 : highway to horror.

PN6728 .R68 2002
813.54 [Fic]

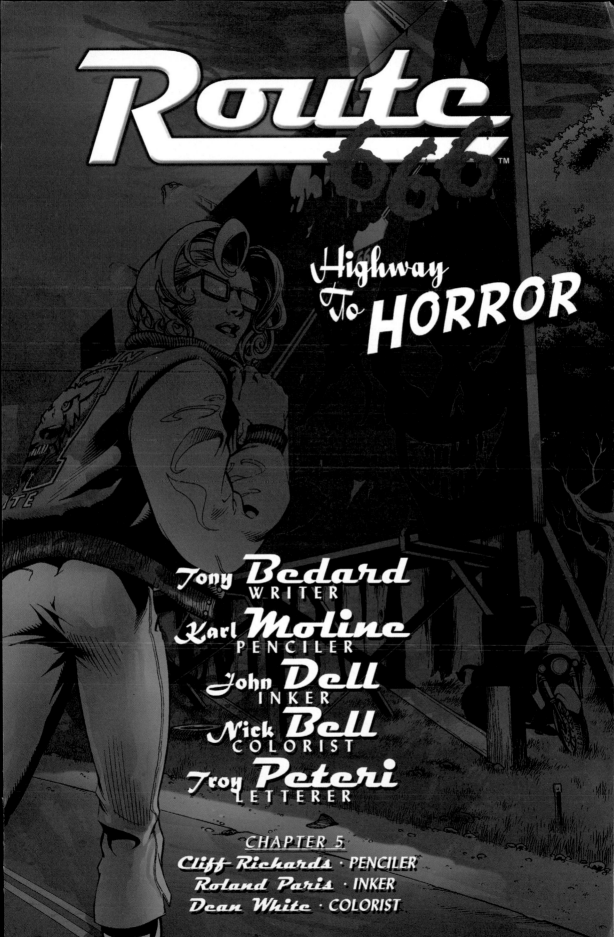

Route 666

Highway to HORROR

Tony **Bedard**
WRITER

Karl **Moline**
PENCILER

John **Dell**
INKER

Nick **Bell**
COLORIST

Troy **Peteri**
LETTERER

CHAPTER 5
Cliff Richards · PENCILER
Roland Paris · INKER
Dean White · COLORIST

CrossGeneration Comics   Oldsmar, Florida

Highway *To* **HORROR**

features Chapters 1 - 6
of the ongoing series
ROUTE 666

Greetings From... WELKIN STATE UNIVERSITY

The Welkin State Campus

WELKIN STATE GYMNASTICS

Beautiful Downtown Plainsville

Dear Mr. & Mrs. Starkweather,

WSU Campus Administration wishes to update you on the status of your daughter Cassandra as it pertains to the special purview of this office. Pursuant to information in your daughter's medical history, the Dean of Students requires us to periodically review Cassie's adjustment to her classes and campus living.

Our caseworker is pleased to report that Cassie seems perfectly normal and is doing well academically. Her friend and roommate, Helene Mengert, is deemed a positive influence, as is Cassie's involvement in our nationally recognized gymnastics program.

Naturally, our inquiry was discreet, considering your daughter's very vocal mistrust of standard counseling techniques. You may choose not to reveal that we checked up on her at all. Please rest assured that Cassie's future at WSU looks every bit as bright as our prospects against Towson College at next weekend's gymnastics meet.

Sincerely,
The WSU Office of Mental Health

"...WHEN I WAS AROUND FIVE, I STARTED GETTING *VISITORS* THAT NO ONE ELSE COULD SEE OR HEAR.

"THEY WOULDN'T HAVE FOUND IT SO CUTE, IF I COULD'VE *DESCRIBED* MY INVISIBLE FRIENDS A LITTLE BETTER.

"THEY'D STICK AROUND FOR AN AFTERNOON, OR A COUPLE OF DAYS, THEN *MOVE ON.*

"MOM AND DAD JUST THOUGHT IT WAS A CUTE LITTLE *PHASE* I WAS GOING THROUGH.

"A LOT OF MY FRIENDS HAD SOME PRETTY BIG 'BOO-BOOS,' BUT THEY DIDN'T SEEM TO MIND, SO NEITHER DID I.

"I DIDN'T KNOW WHY THEY CAME TO *ME* IN PARTICULAR, BUT I COULD TELL THAT THEY *FELT* BETTER AROUND ME.

McLANE FUNERAL HOME

"THIS WENT ON FOR A COUPLE OF YEARS. IT *STOPPED* BEING CUTE THE NIGHT OF MY GRANDFATHER'S FUNERAL."

I SEE.

PLEASE FILL OUT THESE *ADMISSIONS FORMS*, MISTER STARKWEATHER. WE SHALL CHECK IN YOUR DAUGHTER *IMMEDIATELY*.

I'LL CALL YOU EVERY NIGHT, AND WE'LL VISIT EVERY *WEEKEND! PROMISE!*

BYE, MOM.

GUSTAV! HELP THE YOUNG LADY TO HER ROOM.

BYE!

RIGHT THIS WAY, SWEET THING. I'LL GIVE YOU THE *NICKEL* TOUR.

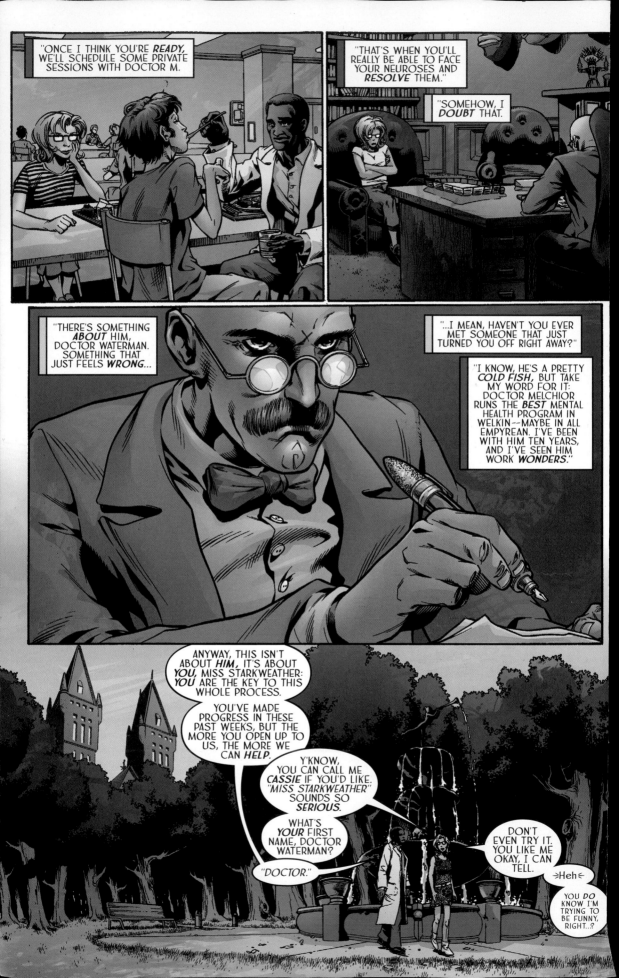

ROUTE 666 · CHAPTER TWO

ROUTE 666 • CHAPTER THREE

ROUTE 666 • CHAPTER FOUR

ROUTE 666 • CHAPTER FIVE

"BUT THERE'S A *REASON* J. ELGAR'S BEEN RUNNING THE N.B.I. EVER SINCE THE GREAT WAR. THE OLD MAN'S *NO FOOL*...

"...HE *KNOWS* THAT IF THIS GIRL'S KILLING SPREE ISN'T ENDED SOON, IT COULD SPARK A NATIONAL *PANIC*.

"SO HE PICKED *ME*, BECAUSE I'LL CHASE EVERY *LEAD*, CALL IN EVERY *FAVOR*, AND DESTROY *ANYONE* WHO KEEPS ME FROM *SNARING* THAT LITTLE *LUNATIC*.

GUNNAR MELCHIOR, MD, PhD
Special Agent-Profiler
Provisional Director
Criminal Psychology Unit
NATIONAL BUREAU of INVESTIGATION

TWN73

"I'VE FOLLOWED HER TRAIL THROUGH FOUR STATES, AND INTERVIEWED EVERYONE WHO'S CROSSED HER PATH. EVERYONE STILL *ALIVE*, THAT IS..."

FORTY-ONE.

...WHAT...?

THE AGENT SAID I ONLY HAD TWENTY-SEVEN KILLS. IT'S FORTY-ONE. *MORE* IF YOU COUNT TONIGHT.

I WANT YOU TO *KNOW*, CASSIE. IT'S IMPORTANT YOU KNOW *ALL* OF IT NOW.

WHERE'D SHE *GO*...?

I *ALWAYS* HAD THESE FEELINGS... THESE *URGES*. IT'S WHY I *ENLISTED* IN THE FIRST PLACE--

-- FIGURED THE SERVICE WAS *MADE* FOR GUYS LIKE ME.

SURE ENOUGH, I MADE A WHIZ-BANG MARINE. BUT WHEN I CAME HOME FROM THE WAR, I DIDN'T *FIT IN*.

AND WHEN I COULDN'T HOLD IT IN ANY MORE, MY DADDY BECAME MY FIRST PEACETIME KILL.

I WONDERED EVER SINCE WHY I WAS *BORN* THIS WAY. WHAT *PURPOSE* WOULD THE GOOD LORD HAVE, PUTTING SUCH THINGS IN MY HEAD?

AND THEN I MEET *YOU*, AND SUDDENLY I *KNOW* MY PURPOSE. YOU CAN SEE THE *REAL* MONSTERS OUT THERE, BUT YOU LOOK AT *ME*, AND YOU *DON'T* SEE A BEAST.

YOU KNOW *WHY*, DON'T YOU? 'CAUSE WE'RE THE *SAME*, YOU AND I. WE WEREN'T MEANT TO FIT IN. WE WERE MEANT FOR SOMETHING GREATER.